Cinderella
Read and Sing

DISNEY PRESS

Los Angeles • New York

For information address Disney Press, 1101 Flower Street, Glendale, California 91201.

ISBN 978-1-4847-0782-1
F383-2370-2-14304
Printed in China
First Edition
1 3 5 7 9 10 8 6 4 2

For more Disney Press fun visit www.disneybooks.com

Contents

Cinderella

Once there was a kind and beautiful girl named Cinderella, who lived with her cruel stepmother and two selfish stepsisters, Anastasia and Drizella. Every morning, Cinderella told her little mouse and bird friends about her dreams. "They're wishes my heart makes when I'm asleep. If I believe in them, someday they'll come true!" she said.

One day, an announcement arrived from the palace. The King was giving a royal ball in honor of the Prince. Every maiden in the kingdom was commanded to come!

Cinderella's stepsisters were thrilled. This was their chance to make the Prince fall in love with them. Cinderella was excited, too. "Every maiden!" she said. "That means I can go, too!"

Cinderella's stepsisters laughed. How could Cinderella expect to go to the ball? But her stepmother smiled slyly.

"You may go, Cinderella," she said. "If you do all your work. And if you find something suitable to wear!"

All that day, Cinderella's stepmother and stepsisters shouted orders at her. Cinderella's mouse and bird friends watched sadly. Cinderella was so kind to them. They wished they could do something for her.

"Poor Cinderelly," said Jaq. "They keeping her so busy, she never get her dress done."

Then the mice had an idea! "We can do it!" they cried.

Soon the mice and birds were happily snipping and stitching to make a lovely dress for Cinderella.

When evening came, a tired Cinderella trudged up the stairs to her tiny attic room. She hadn't had any time to find a dress for the ball. Now she would have to stay home.

Suddenly, Cinderella saw the pretty gown her animal friends had made for her.

"Surprise!" they cried.

Cinderella could hardly speak. "Oh! How can I ever . . . oh, thank you so much!" she said.

Dressed and ready, Cinderella ran downstairs. "Wait! Please! Wait for me!" she called out.

Anastasia and Drizella saw how lovely Cinderella looked and flew into a jealous rage. They ripped her dress to shreds.

"That's enough, girls," Lady Tremaine said at last. "Don't upset yourselves before the ball. It's time to go."

Cinderella was heartbroken. She ran into the garden, weeping. "It's no use. There's nothing left to believe in!" she sobbed.

Suddenly, she heard a cheery voice say, "Nonsense, child. If you didn't believe, I wouldn't be here . . . and here I am!"

Cinderella looked up and saw an older woman smiling at her. "I'm your fairy godmother," the woman said. "Dry your tears. We must hurry!"

With a wave of her wand, the Fairy Godmother turned a pumpkin into a coach and Cinderella's mouse friends into white horses.

The Fairy Godmother hurried Cinderella to her coach. "But . . . but . . . my dress," Cinderella said.

"Yes, yes . . . it's lovely," the Fairy Godmother said. Then she got a good look at Cinderella. "Good heavens, child! You can't go in that. You need a dress. Well, just leave it to me. What a gown this will be!"

At the ball, the Grand Duke and the King watched the Prince greet one maiden after another with a polite but bored expression. Then, suddenly, a hush fell over the ballroom.

The Prince looked toward the grand entrance. The loveliest girl he had ever seen stood on the steps. It was Cinderella.

Prince Charming knew he'd found the girl of his dreams. "May I have this dance?" he asked.

As the music played, the two waltzed around the ballroom and out into the garden.

Soon enough, the castle clock began to chime.

"Oh, my goodness," Cinderella cried. "It's midnight! I must go! Good-bye!"

As Cinderella ran away, the Prince rushed after her. "Wait! Come back!" he called. "I don't even know your name!"

Cinderella darted through the ballroom and raced down the palace steps, losing a glass slipper on the way.

Cinderella jumped into her coach and sped away. As the clock finished chiming, the spell broke. The coach became a pumpkin, the horses turned back into mice, and Cinderella was again dressed in rags.

The next day, the King sent out a royal proclamation. The girl whose foot fit the glass slipper would wed the Prince.

Cinderella couldn't hide her happiness from her stepmother.

"So, Cinderella is the girl the Prince seeks," the Stepmother said. "Well, he'll never find her!" And with that, she locked Cinderella in her attic room.

Before long, the Grand Duke and a royal footman arrived with the glass slipper. The Stepmother and stepsisters smiled their sweetest smiles and ushered them in. Both Anastasia and Drizella were eager to find some way to get their feet to fit the slipper! But though they pushed and shoved, neither of the stepsisters could squeeze a foot into it.

Meanwhile, Cinderella's mouse friends struggled to get the key out of the Stepmother's pocket without her noticing. Then they had to lug it all the way upstairs to the attic. "Thissa way. Up, up, up wif it. Gotta hurry!" they cried.

The mice slid the key beneath Cinderella's door. She was free!

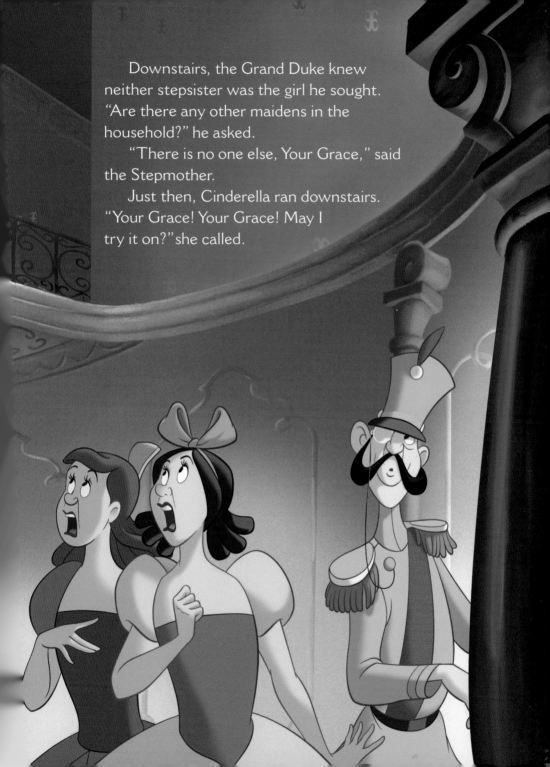

Downstairs, the Grand Duke knew
neither stepsister was the girl he sought.
"Are there any other maidens in the
household?" he asked.

"There is no one else, Your Grace," said
the Stepmother.

Just then, Cinderella ran downstairs.
"Your Grace! Your Grace! May I
try it on?" she called.

As the footman carried the slipper to Cinderella, the Stepmother tripped him, and he fell! The slipper smashed into a hundred pieces. The Grand Duke was horrified!

Cinderella smiled and reached into her pocket. "Perhaps I can help," she said. "You see, I have the other slipper."

The Stepmother and stepsisters gasped. With a low bow, the Grand Duke slipped it onto Cinderella's dainty foot. It fit perfectly!

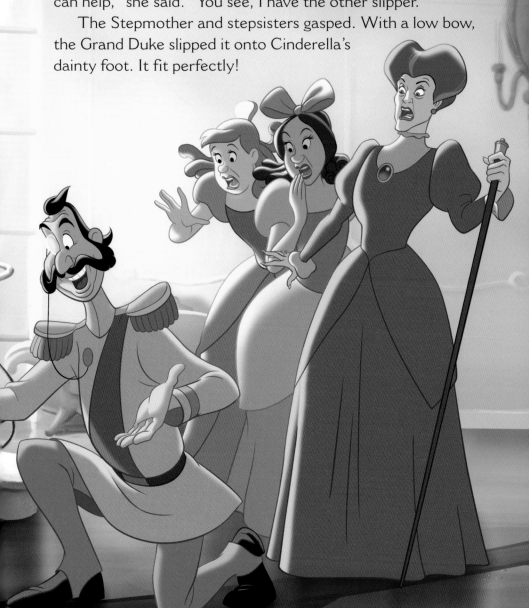

Soon wedding bells rang throughout the kingdom. As the happily married couple rode away in the royal coach, Cinderella realized she had been right, after all. If you keep on believing, your dreams will come true.

And they all lived happily ever after.

Cinderella's Royal Wedding

Cinderella's dream was coming true. She had found her happily ever after. Now she and the Prince were to be married!

The King was thrilled to hear the news. In the hall, he gestured to a portrait of a beautiful woman. "This was my wife on our wedding day. You shall wear the same thing. It is royal family tradition. And there is nothing more important than family traditions!"

"Royal traditions—all you need to know," said the Grand Duke later as he brought Cinderella a stack of books.

Cinderella read and read, trying to remember everything, until at last she fell asleep.

In her dream, Cinderella's mother gave her a special gift. "Cinderella, my love, this necklace will remind you that whenever you have a problem, if you listen to your heart, it will lead you to the answer."

Cinderella woke up, filled with the memory of her mother's love. Getting out of bed, she began to search through some of her old trunks.

"Need some help, dearie?" asked the Fairy Godmother, showing up suddenly in Cinderella's room. So with the help of the Fairy Godmother, the mice, and a little magic, Cinderella found what she was looking for—a portrait of her mother on her wedding day.

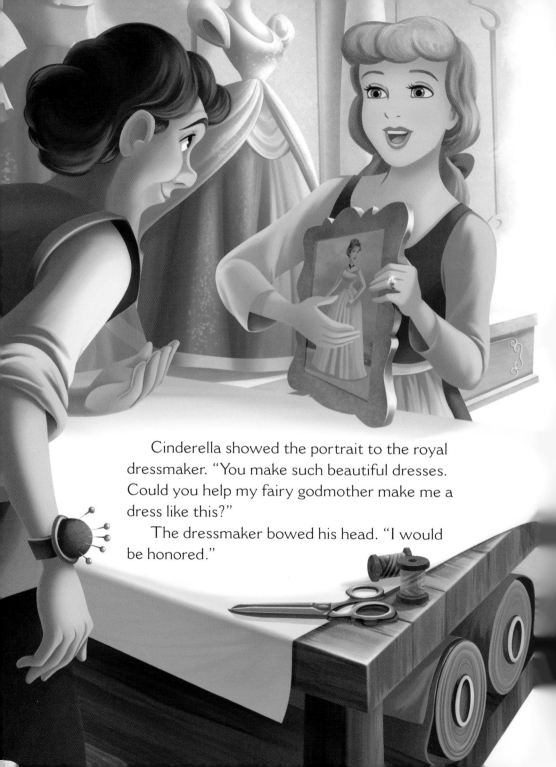

Cinderella showed the portrait to the royal
dressmaker. "You make such beautiful dresses.
Could you help my fairy godmother make me a
dress like this?"

The dressmaker bowed his head. "I would
be honored."

Next Cinderella visited the royal jeweler. "You are an artist. Do you think it would be possible to work with my mouse friends and combine two necklaces into one?"

"For you I shall create the finest necklace in the kingdom."

Finally, the royal wedding day arrived. The King came to see Cinderella.

"I hope you don't mind. This is a copy of my mother's wedding dress," said Cinderella. "It honors my family tradition. And with my necklace and veil, I also honor yours, Your Majesty."

The King saw that his queen's pearls had been used to make the wedding necklace and veil. "Oh, my dear girl, this is a great honor. You have blended the treasures of two families—and created a new tradition for our family."

The King proudly offered
Cinderella his arm. "Let's not
keep the Prince waiting."

A happy King led Cinderella down the aisle. The
guests were thrilled. The Prince was entranced. Even
the Grand Duke wiped a tear from his eye.

The Prince and Cinderella answered the
question that all brides and grooms must
answer.

"They do! They do!" shouted Gus-Gus.

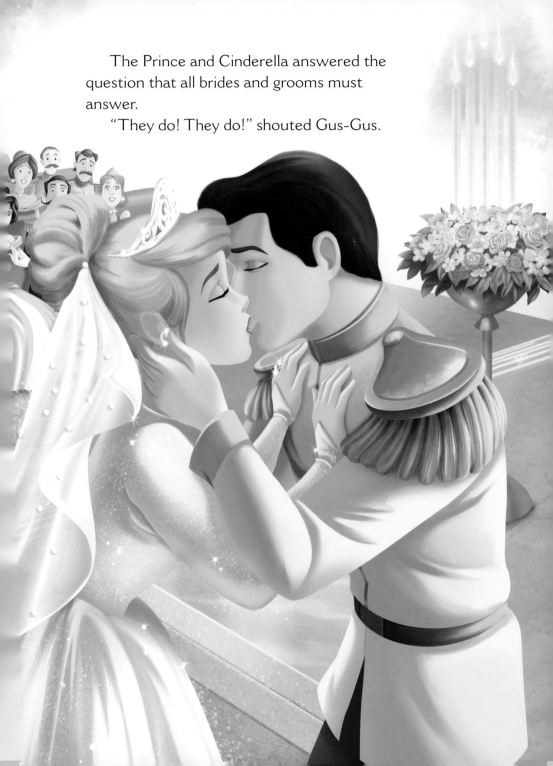

And so it was that by following
tradition—and her heart—Cinderella
had the wedding of her dreams!

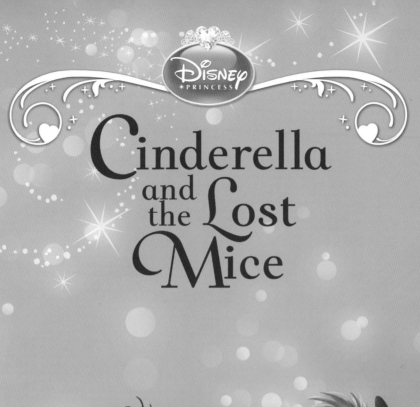

Cinderella
and the Lost
Mice

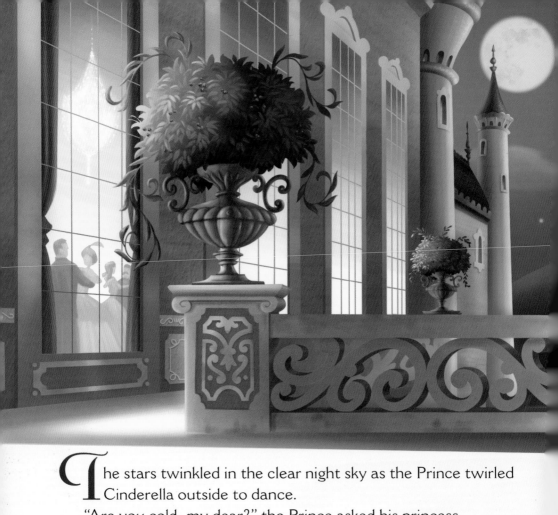

The stars twinkled in the clear night sky as the Prince twirled Cinderella outside to dance.

"Are you cold, my dear?" the Prince asked his princess.

"Just a bit, but—"

Smiling, the Prince reached for a box he had hidden under a bench. Inside was a beautiful winter coat.

"Oh, it's simply lovely!" Cinderella exclaimed. "Thank you!"

The next morning, Cinderella showed her coat to Suzy the mouse. "Nice-a! Nice-a!" Suzy nodded and nuzzled the warm coat.

Cinderella didn't notice that Suzy had just come in from the cold. The tiny mouse was shivering even though the room was warm!

Just then, Gus and Jaq scampered up onto
Cinderella's dressing table.

"Cinderelly! Cinderelly!" they chattered.

Cinderella didn't hear them as she rushed off to meet
the Prince. She didn't know that they were cold, too!

Soon several more cold and shivering mice entered the room. They sat in front of the fire until their teeth stopped chattering. The poor mice had spent the night in the freezing attic! They hoped Cinderella would let them stay in her warm room. But there was a problem.

 53

"Shoo, shoo!" The cruel housekeeper barged into the room and began chasing the mice! "You're making the whole castle dirty!" she shouted. "I should have the gardener haul you away!"

She was the reason the mice were cold—and scared! They stayed in the attic to hide from her!

The mice scrambled back to the chilly attic, not knowing where else to go. "Cinderelly," Gus sighed. They needed her help!

Suddenly—*WHAM!*—the gardener slammed cages over the mice and scooped them up!

"Now take them outside!" shrieked the housekeeper. "Take them far enough away that they never return!"

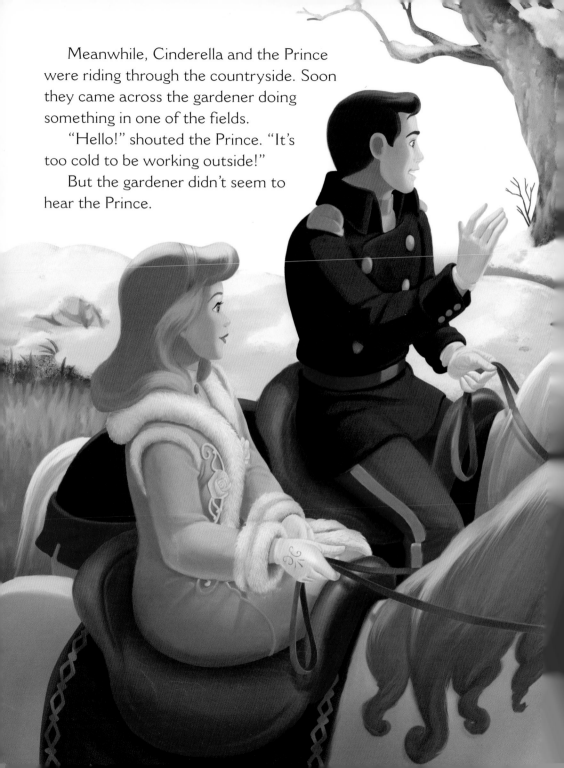

Meanwhile, Cinderella and the Prince were riding through the countryside. Soon they came across the gardener doing something in one of the fields.

"Hello!" shouted the Prince. "It's too cold to be working outside!"

But the gardener didn't seem to hear the Prince.

When the Prince and Cinderella returned to the stables, the Prince asked, "Do you think the gardener was acting oddly?"

"Perhaps he was distracted," Cinderella replied thoughtfully.

But the gardener was not distracted. He was worried about the mice! He knew that they would freeze in the fields.

"Don't mention this to the housekeeper," he told his helpers, "but I want to bring these poor mice to the stables."

So they took the grateful mice to their new home and even fed them.

Inside the castle, Cinderella was looking for her little friends when she ran into the Prince.

"Why, hello!" the Prince said cheerfully. "Are you looking for the same person I am?"

"Person?" asked Cinderella. "Why, no! I'm looking for the mice!"

"Ah," said the Prince. "And I am looking for the housekeeper who apparently threw them out of the castle today. She said they were dirty!"

"Dirty! Oh, no!" Cinderella cried. "They're not dirty. And besides, they'll freeze outside!"

"Don't worry, my dear. The mice have found a new friend." The Prince then told Cinderella about the gardener and what he had done.

Together, Cinderella and the Prince went to the stables, where they found and thanked the gardener. Then Cinderella awakened the mice, who were snuggled comfortably in the horses' manes.

"Cinderelly! Cinderelly!" the mice shouted happily.

A few nights later, there was a grand ball—
with the gardener as the guest of honor. The cruel
housekeeper now peeled potatoes in the kitchen. She
would not be bothering the mice again. Meanwhile, the
mice celebrated with a banquet of their own. And as for the
horses, they got extra apples all around!

Princess in Disguise

Cinderella's life had changed overnight! One day, she was cleaning and cooking for her stepmother and stepsisters. The next day, she was married to the Prince and living in a palace.

Cinderella loved living with the Prince, but it felt strange to have the royal staff waiting on her. She tried to make as little work for them as possible. Sometimes she even made her own bed before they came in.

Cinderella wanted to get to know the royal staff better. She remembered how lonely she'd been at her stepmother's house. She hoped the maids knew that she was their friend. But whenever Cinderella invited them to tea or tried to chat with them, they would politely smile and hurry away to finish other chores.

One morning at breakfast, Cinderella told the Prince that she was worried. "I want to make sure the servants are happy working here," she said. "But I can't seem to get any of them to talk to me."

"Wouldn't they tell us if something was wrong?" the Prince asked.

Cinderella nodded. "I suppose so. I just wish there was a way to know for certain."

Later that morning, Cinderella talked with her mouse friends Jaq and Gus. "There must be something I can do to find out if the staff is happy," she said. "But no one is going to tell me what they really think."

"They would-a talked to you before," Jaq said. "Cinderelly didn't look-a like a princess then."

Suddenly, Cinderella's eyes lit up.

"That's it!" she exclaimed. "Thank you, Jaq!"

Cinderella went into town and bought a wig and a maid's outfit. When she returned to the castle, she looked like a member of the royal staff!

As Cinderella walked down the hall, she came upon a maid carrying a heavy tub of water.

"Let me help with that," Cinderella said, and she helped the maid carry the large tub to the center of the ballroom.

"Do you like working here?" Cinderella asked.

"Well, yes," the maid said. She thought for a moment. "But there are some things I would change."

"Like what?" Cinderella asked.

"Like this tub," the maid replied. "If only it were on wheels!"

"Why don't you suggest it?" Cinderella said.

"Oh, the royal family is very busy," the maid said. "I wouldn't want to bother them."

Next Cinderella headed to the banquet hall. Some of the royal staff members were at a long table. They chatted happily as they polished the silver.

"Come join us!" one of the maids called.

Cinderella walked over and examined the gleaming silver. "This looks like it's been polished already," she said.

"It was, just yesterday," the maid replied. "But we're supposed to polish it every day. Rules are rules."

Just then, Cinderella heard a voice coming from down the hall. It was Prudence, head of the royal housekeeping staff! Cinderella ducked out of sight.

"Excuse me," Prudence said, pulling aside one of the maids. "When you are finished here, I'll need you to polish the backup silver."

Hmmm, Cinderella thought. She wondered if the royal family even knew they *had* backup silver.

When the polishing was finally finished, Cinderella went to the palace's sewing room.

"These are beautiful," Cinderella said, admiring the dresses the seamstresses were making.

"Gowns are my favorite things to sew," one of the seamstresses said. "Each time I finish one, I imagine what it would be like to wear it. Just once I wish we could go to a ball. I would dance and dance all night long."

"What I wish," added another seamstress, "is that we had more light in here. I can barely see the lace I'm stitching!"

Soon it was time for lunch. Cinderella followed the maids to the kitchen. She was delighted to see steaming bowls of soup and big slices of crusty bread laid out on a long table.

But just as everyone sat down, a bell rang. The signal meant that one of the royal staff members was needed for a task. A butler at the end of the table got up. He hadn't even had a chance to taste his soup!

Cinderella knew she had to do something! She raced back toward her room to change into her own clothing. On her way there, she bumped into the Prince.

"Cinderella!" he exclaimed in surprise. "Why ever are you dressed like that?"

Cinderella smiled. "I realized that the only way to make sure the staff was happy was to dress up as a maid myself!" she explained. "They had so many wonderful ideas about how to make the palace a better place to work. I can't wait to tell the King and the Grand Duke all about it."

A short while later, Cinderella and the Prince stood before the King and the Grand Duke.

Cinderella told them all about her adventure as a maid. "I just know we could make things better for the royal staff," she said.

That afternoon, Cinderella gathered the royal staff and explained her deception. The servants looked at one another nervously.

"From now on," Cinderella said, "all the washtubs will be on wheels, the silver will be polished only when it needs to be, more windows will be added to the sewing room, and your meals will no longer be interrupted."

The royal staff was astonished. They were beginning to like this new princess!

The Lost Tiara

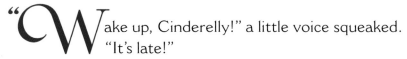

"Wake up, Cinderelly!" a little voice squeaked. "It's late!"

Cinderella sat straight up in bed. "Oh, my goodness!" she said to her mouse friend Gus. "Did I oversleep? I need to make breakfast, and feed the chickens, and start the . . ."

Cinderella's voice trailed off as she looked around. Instead of being in a drafty old attic, she was in a large, bright, and sunny room.

Cinderella breathed a sigh of relief. She was a princess now. She had left her old life behind when she married the Prince. "It's okay, Gus-Gus," she said. "Sometimes I forget that I don't have to wake up to do my chores, too!"

Cinderella stretched and got out of bed. Peering into her wardrobe, she gazed at the hundreds of dresses inside. Finally, she pulled out two and held them up. "Which one should I wear today?" she asked her mouse friends.

Cinderella quickly dressed and then headed down to the dining room. The King and the Prince were already downstairs. The King was reading a letter, and he looked upset.

"What's wrong?" Cinderella asked. "Have you received bad news?"

The King handed Cinderella the letter.

My dear family,

It has been far too long since I last saw you. And I can hardly wait to meet the newest addition to the family— Cinderella! I arrive Wednesday in the late afternoon. Please have my usual rooms ready.

Love always,

Grandmama

"I don't understand," Cinderella said. "This seems like good news!"

"It is," said the King. "She arrives this very evening. But I am upset because we won't be here to greet her. We are scheduled for a visit with a neighboring kingdom."

"Cinderella will be here," the Prince said. Then he turned to his bride. "You and Grandmama will be able to spend some time getting to know each other. By the time Father and I get back, you are sure to be the dearest of friends!"

Cinderella nodded. She was eager to meet the Prince's grandmother, but she was also nervous. What if she didn't like Cinderella?

"Well, we'd best be off," said the King suddenly. "Our coach awaits."

Cinderella walked outside with the Prince. "Don't forget to wear the tiara Grandmama sent you," the Prince called as he climbed into the coach. Cinderella nodded and waved good-bye. Then she hurried back inside. She was late for a meeting with the royal dressmaker!

When Cinderella pushed open the drawing-room door, she found Chloe, the royal dressmaker, unpacking her dresses. Cinderella was going to the theater the next day, and she needed a new gown.

One by one, Cinderella tried on Chloe's creations. There were pinks and greens and blues and yellows. Each dress was beautiful and unique.

Finally, Cinderella selected one that felt just right.

Trying on so many dresses had made Cinderella hungry. Gathering a picnic basket and a blanket, the princess laid out lunch for her and her mouse friends in the garden.

Cinderella loved living at the castle with the Prince, but being a princess could be a lot of work. She was always happy when she could find time to do simple things like spend time with her friends. And her friends enjoyed it, too!

As Cinderella gazed around the garden, she had an idea. "I know just how to welcome Grandmama," she said. "I'll make a lovely bouquet for her!"

Cinderella hurried inside to get her gardening shears and a vase. Soon she was picking a lovely selection of flowers . . . violets, tulips, peonies, and red, red roses!

"Perfect!" she said when the bouquet was complete.

Cinderella handed the vase to a footman to put in Grandmama's room. Then she and her mouse friends went to find the tiara Grandmama had given her.

Cinderella knew the royal jewels were kept in the Royal Jewel Vault, but she had never been there. Stepping inside, she could hardly believe her eyes. She had never seen so many jewels in her entire life!

"I am looking for a tiara the Prince's grandmama gave me," Cinderella told Pierre, the royal jeweler.

As Pierre hurried to find the tiara, Cinderella examined the jewels. Picking up a beautiful necklace, she put it on.

"Look at this-a," said Jaq, holding up a purple earring.

Cinderella was just about to try on the earring when Pierre returned with the tiara case. He looked very upset. "I'm sorry, Princess," Pierre said. "But the case is empty!"

"Oh, my!" said Cinderella.

"Don't worry, Cinderelly," said Gus. "We'll find it!"

Cinderella nodded, and she and her mouse friends set off to search the castle. They were looking in the parlor when the door creaked open. It was the housekeeper. "Oh, my goodness!" she gasped when she spotted the princess peering beneath a rug.

Cinderella looked up. "Hello!" she cried. Then, thinking quickly, she added, "I'm just playing a game with the mice!"

The housekeeper gave Cinderella a strange smile and then continued on her way.

It soon became clear that the tiara was not in the parlor. Cinderella and her friends moved on to the kitchen, but it was not there, either. It was not in the ballroom or the dining room or even the garden.

Suddenly, the grandfather clock bonged. Cinderella gasped. Grandmama would be arriving any moment, and Cinderella was covered in dirt! She had to get ready!

Racing back inside, Cinderella nearly smacked into Gus. "Cinderelly!" the mouse cried. "There's someone in your bedroom. And she's going through your jewelry box!"

Cinderella gasped and ran down the hall to her bedroom. Without a second thought, she threw open the door to her room. "Is anyone there?" she cried out.

Inside were three castle guards. They were laughing and joking with a sweet-looking older woman. "A thousand pardons, Your Highness," a guard said. "We heard strange noises coming from the princess's room."

The woman laughed. "No, it is all my fault. Imagine, getting lost in my own home!" Then she turned to Cinderella. "You must be my new granddaughter," she said.

Cinderella smiled and began to say hello when Grandmama
interrupted her.

"So where is the tiara I sent you?" she asked.

Cinderella gulped. "Ummm . . . you'll see it soon," she said.

Grandmama frowned and clutched her large purse closer
to her side. "Such a disappointment. I had better head to my
room, then," she said.

Cinderella nodded and started to walk away. Then she
stopped and turned back. She was about to speak when she
saw Grandmama shove the vase of flowers at a footman.
"Who would put flowers in my room? Don't you know I'm
allergic?" she cried.

The next day, Cinderella invited Grandmama to go with her to the theater.

"Oh, what a lovely idea!" Grandmama said. "I haven't been to the theater in ages!"

All the way there, Cinderella tried to think of things to talk to Grandmama about. Things other than tiaras and flowers! But Cinderella could think of nothing. And it seemed that Grandmama had nothing to say, either.

In the Royal Box, Grandmama squinted at her program. With a frown, she began to root around in her bag. "I know my glasses are in here somewhere. . . ."

Cinderella reached for the bag. "Let me help you," she offered.

Grandmama snatched the bag away. "I can do it myself!"

"I'm sorry," said Cinderella. She seemed to do everything wrong when it came to Grandmama!

Suddenly, Cinderella looked down at the stage and gasped. The star of the show was wearing the missing tiara!

Luckily, the actress quickly left the stage and changed her costume. When the show was over, Cinderella ushered Grandmama out for tea. She would come back later for the tiara.

But things did not go smoothly at the salon. Gus, who had been sleeping in Cinderella's bag, smelled the pastries and popped out for a bite.

"*Eek!* A mouse!" Grandmama cried.

"This is my friend Gus," Cinderella explained. She expected Grandmama to be upset, but instead, she lifted her teacup.

"Pleased to meet you!" she told Gus.

Cinderella, Gus, and Grandmama finished their tea and then returned to their carriage.

"Would you mind stopping at the theater on the way home?" Cinderella asked. "I . . . uh . . . left something there accidentally."

Grandmama graciously agreed, and Cinderella raced inside to find the prop master. She still did not know how the tiara had ended up at the theater. She just knew she had to get it back.

"Oh, my," said the prop master. "I'm afraid that tiara was accidentally ruined after the show! We threw it away."

Cinderella knew it was time to tell Grandmama the truth.

"I . . . I . . . I lost the tiara you sent me," said Cinderella when she returned to the carriage. "And I've been trying to keep it from you since you arrived." Cinderella hung her head with shame.

Grandmama looked very, very surprised. In fact, she was speechless. Then she started to laugh. "Actually, there is something I have been meaning to tell you," she said.

Before Grandmama could say another word, Cinderella cried out, "Stop the carriage!"

On the sidewalk, a little girl was crying. Cinderella climbed out of the carriage and walked over to the little girl. "What is wrong?" she asked.

"A mean boy stole my crown," the girl said. "And he put it where I can't reach it. See?" The little girl pointed to a statue of the King in the courtyard. On his head was Cinderella's tiara! Grandmama had joined them by this time. Looking up, she began to laugh again.

Cinderella looked at Grandmama. Why was she laughing when the precious tiara was on a statue of the King?

"Cinderella," Grandmama said, "it is time for me to be honest with you. That tiara is a fake!" Opening her bag, Grandmama pulled out a matching tiara.

"I did not have time to have a real one made for you before your wedding," she explained. "So I sent you a fake tiara. I was hoping to exchange it for this one without you ever knowing!"

Cinderella joined in Grandmama's laughter. "What silly people we both are, trying to keep our secrets!"

When Cinderella stopped laughing, she took the tiara from Grandmama. "Now may I try it on?" she said.

Cinderella placed the tiara on her head. "Oh, it is beautiful," said Grandmama, "just as I knew it would be."

Cinderella smiled and the two women started laughing again. Just at that moment, the Prince's carriage pulled into the square.

"Why, what is so funny?" he asked Cinderella. "And why is my father's statue wearing a tiara?"

But Cinderella and Grandmama could only laugh. Cinderella smiled. She knew this was the first of many adventures she would have with her new grandmama!

A New Mouse

"Who wants crumpets and strawberries?" Cinderella asked. She was having breakfast with her mouse friends.

"Me, me!" Gus cried.

"Thank you, Cinderelly!" Jaq said.

Just then, a royal page stepped into the room. "Madame Laurent has arrived."

Madame Laurent was the Prince's cousin, who was visiting from far away.

Cinderella was nervous. She had never met Madame Laurent. What if she didn't like Cinderella?

Madame Laurent swept in. "You must be Cinderella," she said as she hugged the princess. "I've heard so much about you!"

Cinderella smiled and breathed a sigh of relief. It seemed that Madame Laurent was quite sweet.

"Psst!" Jaq said. He grabbed Gus's arm and pointed to a fancy little house that Madame Laurent had brought with her. It looked just perfect for a mouse to live in.

Curious, they crept toward it.

Jaq and Gus were still creeping toward the house when Madame Laurent leaned down and picked it up.

"Cinderella," Madame Laurent said. "Allow me to introduce my beloved friend Babette."

She opened the door to the house and Babette walked onto her hand.

Jaq and Gus couldn't believe it. Babette was a mouse! Gus waved, but Babette just stared at them.

"Would you like a crumpet, Babette?" Cinderella asked. The mouse took a piece and ran back into her house.

"She should have said 'thank you,'" Jaq whispered
to Gus.

"Rude!" Gus agreed.

"How about a tour of the castle?" Madame Laurent said, and took Cinderella by the arm.

"Jaq, Gus, perhaps you can give Babette a tour, too," Cinderella suggested.

"This is the library!" Jaq said.
"Lotsa books," Gus said, pointing.
Babette looked around but didn't say a word.

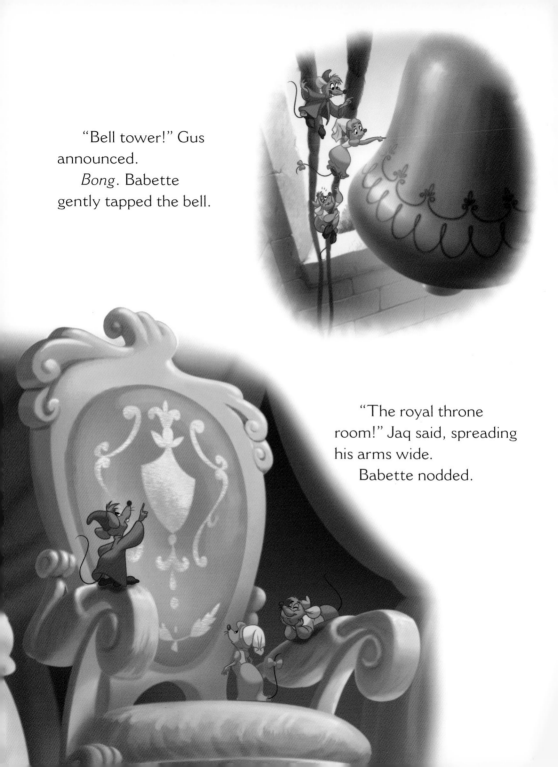

"Bell tower!" Gus
announced.
Bong. Babette
gently tapped the bell.

"The royal throne
room!" Jaq said, spreading
his arms wide.
Babette nodded.

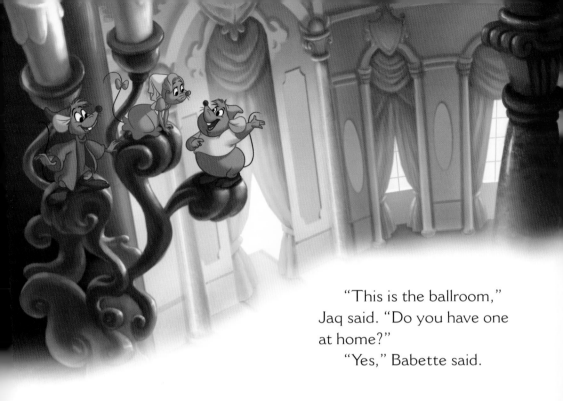

"This is the ballroom,"
Jaq said. "Do you have one
at home?"

"Yes," Babette said.

Gus and Jaq looked at
each other. Babette was
no fun.

"Babette! What a snob," Jaq told Cinderella later.

"Stuck up!" Gus agreed.

"Now, now," Cinderella said gently. "You hardly know her. Give her a chance." Cinderella's mother had taught her to be kind to everyone, no matter how they behaved.

Just then, Cinderella glanced down at her bare wrist.
"My bracelet!" she gasped. "It must have fallen off during
Madame Laurent's tour."
"We'll help you find it, Cinderelly!" Jaq cried.

They went to Madame Laurent first. But she hadn't seen the bracelet.

"I can help you look," a soft voice said. It was Babette, stepping out from her little house.

The three mice scurried from room to room. They looked behind curtains, on top of cabinets, and even in the tearoom.

"Jaq! Gus!" Babette cried.
They hurried over to her.
Babette had found Cinderella's bracelet!

"Tell Cinderelly!" Gus said.

"Oh, I couldn't!" Babette said, blushing. Suddenly, Jaq understood: Babette wasn't a snob. She was just shy!

"Be brave!" Gus said. He and Jaq took her to find Cinderella.

Cinderella was delighted to have her bracelet back. "Thank you, Babette!" she said. "You must have very sharp eyes."

Babette blushed again.

"You saved the day!" Jaq said.

Gus had a wonderful idea. He grabbed Babette's paw.
"Hide-and-seek!" he squeaked.
The three new friends ran off to play.

When Madame Laurent's visit was over, Jaq and Gus were very sorry to say good-bye to Babette.

"Come back soon!" Gus said.

Babette waved. "I'll miss you!" she said.

When the carriage was out of sight, Jaq turned to Cinderella.

"Babette!" he said. "She's so much fun."

"The best!" Gus chimed in.

Cinderella smiled. "I agree," she said.